W9-BQW-061

MISS FISHLEY AFLOAT

For Will
T.S.

For my family
and my friends
E.P.

Kids Can Press Ltd. acknowledges with appreciation the assistance
of the Canada Council and the Ontario Arts Council in the production
of this book.

Canadian Cataloguing in Publication Data

Staunton, Ted 1956 —
  Miss Fishley afloat

ISBN 1-55074-002-4

I. Parker, Eric.   II. Title.

PS8587.T38M58   1990   jC813'.54   C89-090558-4
PZ7.S72Mi   1990

Text copyright ©1990 by Ted Staunton
Illustrations copyright ©1990 by Eric Parker

All rights reserved. No part of this publication may be reproduced,
stored in a retrieval system, or transmitted in any form or by any
means, electronic, mechanical, photocopying, recording or other-
wise without the prior written permission of Kids Can Press Ltd.,
585½ Bloor Street West, Toronto, Ontario, Canada, M6G 1K5.

Book design by N.R. Jackson
Printed and bound in Hong Kong by Everbest Co., Ltd.

90   0   9   8   7   6   5   4   3   2   1

MISS FISHLEY AFLOAT

Written by Ted Staunton
Illustrated by Eric Parker

KIDS CAN PRESS LTD.
Toronto

Last Saturday we biked over to Miss Fishley's cottage at Grumpkin-on-Scone. She treated us to seaweed tea and eels on toast, and told smashing tales of her days on the high seas.

Her neighbours, Commodore Stoat and Nelson, spied from their garden and then snuck up on our bicycles. Miss Fishley ordered the Commodore to push off or she'd feed him raw eels.

The Commodore turned green.

Miss Fishley called him an old mackerel and told us he couldn't stand eels, bicycles or her.

"And d'you know why?" she chuckled. "Because of the time I saved the day by knowing my way about a wheel."

Commodore Stoat pretended not to listen, but he harrumphed in a not-believing sort of way from amongst his roses.

Miss Fishley poured more tea and began:

Knee high to a sea-horse I was, and cabin girl on my father's ship, the *Esmeralda*. We ferried fence posts to fish farmers up and down the coast. "Fishley's Folly" the old salts called her, for she was slow as snails.

But not a sailor in Grumpkin was laughing the day we took on a new cargo bound for across the sea — great cork-lined crates stamped Emerald Flash, Sapphire Star, Diamond Special and Ruby Rocket, from the Crown Jewel Company in Hardride, Spokeshire.

Soon all Grumpkin was talking of treasure, and right they were. For a true Fishley knows her cargo, and I'd peeked inside those crates.

We cast off smooth as silk. I took the
wheel for the first tricky turns. All hands cheered,
except for Algernon, the ship's boy, who was seasick. He'd
turned green as seaweed before we'd weighed anchor, so we dubbed
him "Algy."

And a slippery bit of something he was, too. Algy'd got the boot
from fourteen schools in a row, so he was packed off to sea by
his family.

"The boy don't know a poop deck from a periwinkle," the crew
growled. "Slower than a sea turtle on a sand bar."

Well, Algy was slow but the *Esmeralda* was slower, and the typhoon
season was coming on. I tried to keep things cheery with yarns and
hornpipes, but the crew fretted and Captain Fishley near chewed
through his pipe with worry.

"Neptunia," said he to me, "we're done for if we lose this cargo.
Keep a weather eye cocked for storms."

But 'twas no typhoon that caught us.
Early next morning we heard, "*Esmeralda*! Ahoy!" A ship was coming up fast, filled to the gills with school boys.

"Help!" they called. "We've gone boating on the river and been swept out to sea!"

Now the Captain was always one to lend a hand. He stopped the *Esmeralda* so they could come alongside. Ah, but there was something amiss about these lads, I thought. They had great hairy arms, great hairy legs and great hairy faces — with earrings. The Captain called for his spyglass, but it had disappeared. Closer still the schoolboys came, until I saw the trap.

"Pirates!" I cried.

"Full steam ahead!" thundered the Captain, and I raced to the engine room to help shovel coal. The *Ezzy* puffed till her plates were popping, but those buccaneers leaped aboard before you could say Davey Jones. We were captured in the blink of an eye.

Then up popped a head from a lifeboat. "Are the messy bits done?" asked Algy. "Right then, as pirate captain, I'm in charge. Avast and all that, for I've tricked you. I laid the plan, stole the spy-glass, and left a trail of notes in bottles for my cut-throat crew."

"You thieving little jellyfish," I snarled.

"Tut-tut," he clucked, and jumped behind a pirate.

I kicked the pirate on the shins and sent him hopping. Algy jumped behind another one.

"Why'd you do it?" I roared.

"Bad luck at cards," he sighed, "at the last five schools. I'm stony broke. Now hand over those diamonds and sapphires!"

In a flash the crates were on deck.

"Wot's this?" a pirate gargled. "Them ain't jewels, them's —"

"Bicycles," said I, "from the Crown Jewel Bicycle Company in Hardride, Spokeshire. Ain't they grand?"

A howl went up like a Force Five gale. We'd be walking the plank for sure, unless...Aha!

I climbed aboard a Ruby Rocket and set my course for the main hatch. Everything stopped.

"No hands," I said. They gasped.

"Backwards!" They clapped.

"One foot!" They cheered.

I hopped off and sniffed. "Any swab as can't do that is a lubber!"

Spoken like a true Fishley — and it worked. Every sea-dog aboard
leaped for a crate. What a sight! They pedalled about, trying tricks
and grinning like porpoises — except Algy, whose cutlass caught
in his spokes. Even the Captain gave us a wheelstand across the
poop deck.

Ah, but my plan worked too well. Not one of us noticed the sea grow smooth as glass, or felt the wind fall away, or saw the cloud... growing bigger... and bigger.

Then the typhoon struck.

The *Esmeralda* gave a leap and a lurch and we were tossed like matchsticks through the air and into the sea. I plunked down on a bit of crate, still aboard my Ruby Rocket. I rode out waves like mountains, pedalling up one side and braking down the other. When the blow was over, my tires were worn clean away and the ships had sunk like stones.

But were we finished? Of course not. We lashed together a raft of crates and wooden legs and hung Algy up to dry. Captain Fishley took command.

Up went a sail of pirate bandannas, but the typhoon had left us becalmed. We drifted for days. I practised my handlebar headstand, but the crew muttered and sharpened knives that flashed like piranha's teeth.

One afternoon tempers flared hot as the sun. I heard a roar.

"You snivelling, slime-fingered son of a seacook," the stoker thundered. "Cheat at Go Fish, will ye? Feed 'im to the sharks!"

A second later Algy shot by on a Sapphire Star, the crew close behind. Algy was faster but there was no place to ride. They hoisted him then and there.

"Neptunia," he bawled, "pity a poor lubber! Have a heart like a true Fishley!"

Now I'd as soon they'd keel-hauled the little squid, but the sight of Algy on that Sapphire Star reminded me of my own ride during the typhoon. A wonderful idea swam into my brain and we'd need all hands to make it work.

"Stow that!" I cried. "I've hooked the thing to save us all." I sang out my orders like the Captain himself — and right proud of me he was, too. "Ropes to larboard! Planks to starboard! Lash those barrels! Pass those wheels! Steady as she goes!"

In no time at all, we'd made the first pedal-powered paddle-wheeler
on the Seven Seas. The Captain set a course for home, I gave out
with a shanty to set our pace, and the crew gave me three cheers —
except Algy, of course. Pedalling made him green.

Three days we rode and then we heard a droning on the wind —
a flying machine trailing a banner for Dr. McSwab's Seasick Salts for
Sailors. I flashed an SOS. "Will go for help," they flashed back
and dropped a sample packet of seasick salts. We gave the salts to
Algy, the Captain broke out the last of the ginger beer, and we
pedalled harder than ever! All except Algy. He drank too much
and turned green.

But no rescue came. Night and day we pedalled until, at last, we could pedal no more. There was nothing to eat but one soggy cracker and half a squeezed grape. Sharks circled the raft. We were done for. I'd never skipper my own ship like a true Fishley.

And then, when all seemed lost, I spied a speck in the sky. A bird? Another typhoon? No, it grew into a great silver airship, gliding straight towards us. Soon they were overhead with a message reeling down on a cable:

CAPTAIN FISHLEY AND CREW SOMEWHERE AT SEA.....
CROWN JEWEL BICYCLE COMPANY OFFERS GOLD TO ALL WHO PEDAL RAFT POWERED BY CROWN JEWEL BICYCLES ALL THE WAY TO GRUMPKIN-ON-SCONE.
THE WORLD IS WATCHING. PLEASE ADVISE AT ONCE!
Silas Spoke
SILAS B. SPOKE
CROWN JEWEL COMPANY

"Well, mates," boomed the Captain. "Can we do it?"

Bless my barnacles! Of course we could.

We raised a shout and baskets came down from the airship, filled with fixings for us and oil for the bicycles.

The rest of that voyage was a first-class cruise. We had Ping-Pong on deck, stuffed ourselves with kippers and cakes, and sat for the illustrated papers.

And didn't they cheer when we pedalled into Grumpkin-on-Scone, bold as brass!

There were speeches and cheers and a fortune for all. The pirates got pardons and new bicycles. The Captain and crew got a new ship to carry Crown Jewel bicycles. I got a medal and Algy got sent to his room with no supper.

Miss Fishley passed the last two eels on toast while Commodore Stoat harrumphed about cheating at Go Fish.

"But what happened then?" we asked.

"The Captain sailed soon after," said Miss Fishley. "I stayed in dry dock for school and taught knots at the marine academy on half-holidays. The pirates launched a water-taxi and paddle-boat company. Algy told his family he hated the sea —"

Harrumph!

"– so they stuck him in the Navy –"

Another harrumph.

"– and he grew up to be Commodore Stoat."

A huge harrumph.

Miss Fishley emptied the teapot out the window. There was a squawk from the garden.

"Good for the roses," she snapped. "And now it's time for us to ship out."

Someone had let the air out of our tires. We pumped them up at
Miss Fishley's gate. Miss Fishley stepped the mast on her handlebars,
tested the breeze, and put on sail.

"Now, set a course for home," she ordered us, and she was off with
the wind, riding no-hands around the corner to the sea.

Commodore Stoat cried, "Codswallop!" and slammed his door.

We pedalled slowly home past the Jolly Roger Water Taxi Company. The crew had great hairy arms, great hairy legs and great hairy faces — with earrings.

They were toasting crumpets on a cutlass.